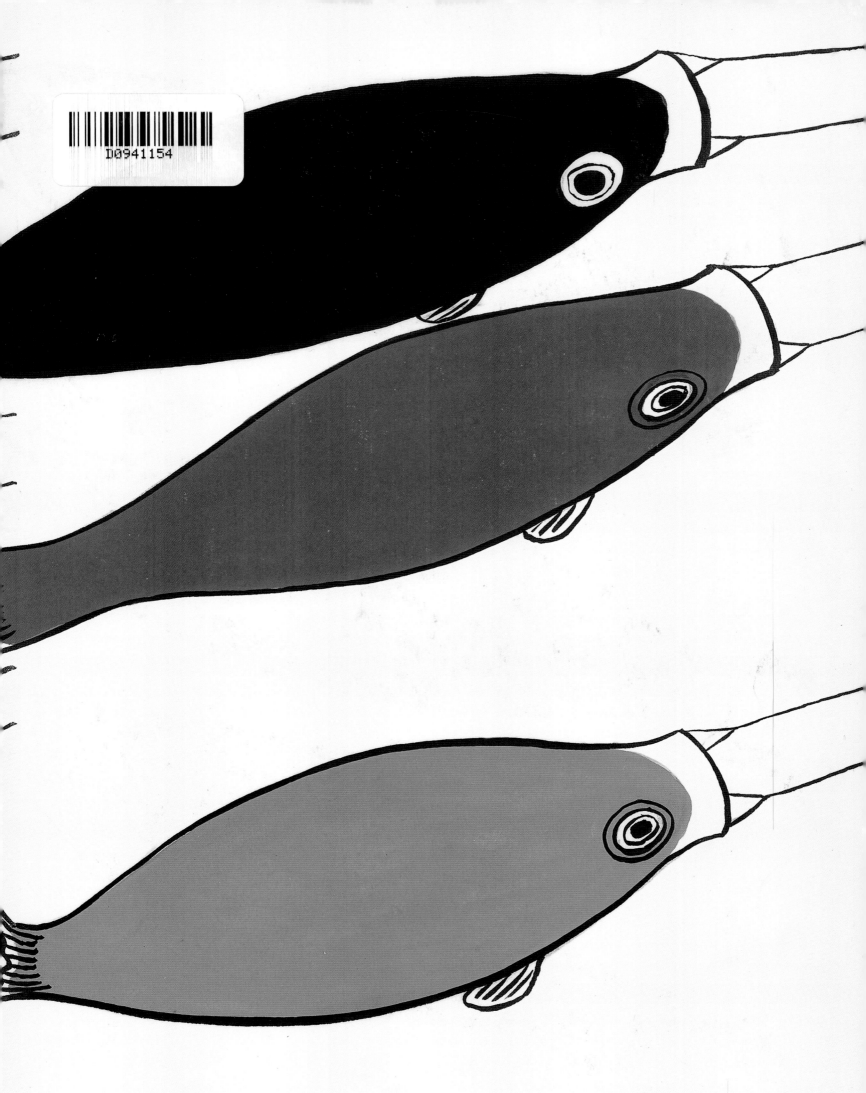

For all the little Naokis of the world …
In memory of my grandfather Pierre,
the ceramist, who loved Japan so much …
V. M.

For my Véronique,
the great wave filled with love.
B. P.

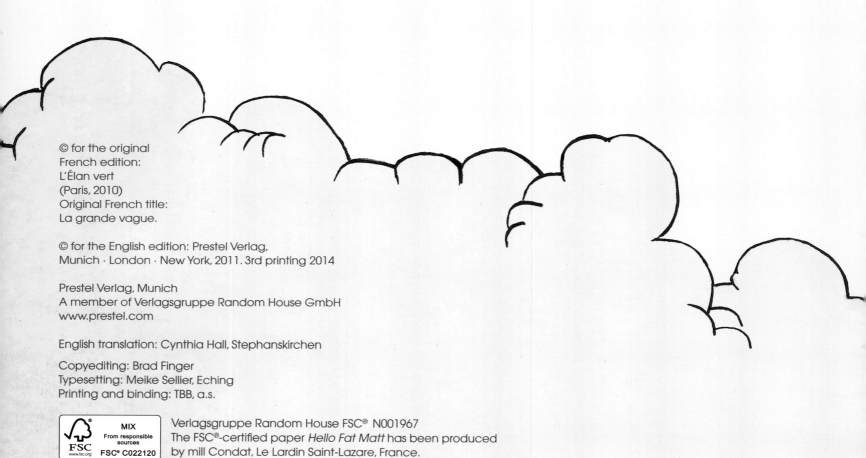

© for the original
French edition:
L'Élan vert
(Paris, 2010)
Original French title:
La grande vague.

© for the English edition: Prestel Verlag,
Munich · London · New York, 2011. 3rd printing 2014

Prestel Verlag, Munich
A member of Verlagsgruppe Random House GmbH
www.prestel.com

English translation: Cynthia Hall, Stephanskirchen

Copyediting: Brad Finger
Typesetting: Meike Sellier, Eching
Printing and binding: TBB, a.s.

Verlagsgruppe Random House FSC® N001967
The FSC®-certified paper *Hello Fat Matt* has been produced
by mill Condat, Le Lardin Saint-Lazare, France.

Printed in Slovakia.

ISBN 978-3-7913-7058-3

The Great Wave

Inspired by a woodcut by Hokusai

Text by Véronique Massenot
Illustrations by Bruno Pilorget

Prestel

Munich · London · New York

Aki and Taro were childless. The summer of their lives
was nearing an end, but they had neither a boy nor girl
to give them joy.
The couple had waited very long, and they had tried
everything they knew to have a child.
They had eaten countless herbs and special foods;
and they had prayed fervently and given offerings
in the temple. At last, they felt their hope was gone.
The child they had so desired did not come.
There were many nights of tears and sorrow ...

but then, suddenly, a miracle.

It happened on an icy cold day in winter.
The wind raged over the sea and threw mighty waves upon the land.
But the men of the village still had to go out
to catch fish. For winter was the season of hunger,
and no fish meant even less to eat.

Three long ships set out from the harbor.
Together they fought the stormy surf,
ascending wave after wave to the crests
and falling back again into the troughs.
The men advanced in this way, wave upon wave,
waiting for the right moment.
They had fish to catch, whatever the cost.

Then, just as they prepared to throw out their nets,
an enormous wave rose up in front of them.
It rose like a gigantic creature opening its foamy mouth,
greedily swallowing up everything before it:
fishermen, nets, boats, everything!

The men held their breath in fear,
clinging to the ships
and ducking down.
Some even closed their eyes.

When they looked out again, the wave had broken.
The brave fishing group had been spared.
Soon the sea became as calm as the men's silent relief.
But this quiet was penetrated by a small, angry cry;
and Taro was heard to shout:

"Look! That wet bundle there is a child! A brand new life!
The wave has set it down in our boat!"

Taro's heart beat more wildly than all the drums of the world together.
He took the baby boy in his arms, and the crying child fell silent.

Taro smiled.
The child, so long awaited and so long hoped for,
had arrived at last.

The happy years passed. Naoki, the boy from the sea,
had a mighty appetite. He ate bowl after bowl
of delicious rice, yet he did not grow any bigger.

Now his seventh birthday was drawing near,
and he'd barely grown an inch.

Aki was worried:
"Would he always stay so small?"
And Taro often thought:
"How could he ever become a proper fisherman?"

But the wise parents had come to know patience.
Maybe their child did not want to grow?
Maybe they only had to wait a little longer?
Wasn't it a great joy just
to hold such a tiny life in their arms?

Naoki waited to grow as well...
while all of his friends shot upwards,
faster than bamboo.

The boy often sat on the trunk of an old pine tree
that stretched its branches out over the water.
As he sat, Naoki's thoughts drifted across the sea,
coming and going like the water's ebb and flow.
The thoughts tormented him with hundreds of questions ...

"Why am I not like the other children?"
"Why did I not come from my mother's belly?"
"Did a woman or a mysterious wave bring me into this world?"
"Who is my 'real' father, who is my mother?"
"Whom should I truly love?"

One day, as he was sitting on his tree trunk, Naoki spied a beautiful fish
beneath him. Its scales shimmered like silver, and it swam back and forth excitedly,
as if wanting to speak.

The boy leaned down … and the fish smiled at him!
He leaned down further … and the fish called out his name!
Then Naoki leaned as far as he could …
and fell headfirst into the sea!

Underwater the fish seemed enormous.
Its impressive whiskers were curly and black, and its voice rich and strong:
"Hello, little man! Come with me, I know who can answer
your questions."

Naoki swam behind him as if he too had fins …

As the boy and the fish got farther from shore,
their surroundings changed.
The water became darker and colder,
and the current stronger and stronger.
Naoki clung tightly to his friend just to keep going.

"I thought everything was nice and calm under the sea,"
the boy said to himself. "I thought you could collect coral,
hide among the water lilies, play with starfish …
and find lost treasure."

But the silent fish could not hear Naoki's thoughts,
and the two dived deeper and deeper
into the dark underwater world.

Then without warning they plunged into a whirlpool,
and Naoki was seized with panic. With all his might
the boy pulled at the fins of his scaly companion.
The fish reared up and swam more slowly,
at last coming to a stop.
"Where are you bringing me? I don't want to go further!
I'm cold and I'm scared! Please turn around,
my parents might be worried.
I want to go back to them … and quickly too!"

At these words, the animal's silver scales trembled and
shone with joy. The back of the fish lengthened
and began to move like a wave. Its body became larger
and larger, sprouting mighty feet with sharp golden claws
from its fins … The fish had turned into a dragon.
"Hold on tight!" roared the dragon.

With a single blow of its tail, the dragon thrust itself
out of the ocean, flew over the volcano,
and placed the boy gently upon his dearly loved beach.
"Goodbye, my friend!" he said
from a cloud above the sea.
"Go now, you no longer need me."

Naoki did not speak. As soon as he felt the sand beneath his feet,
he began to run. The happy boy ran and ran ...
all the way to his parents' house.

When he finally reached home, Naoki turned around
to thank his noble friend.
But the dragon was gone. The sea was as smooth as glass,
as if nothing had happened.

Now it is spring, and today is *Koï Nobori* ... a children's festival.

A thousand and one carp fish float in the wind,
their bodies made of humble cloth.

Naoki looks proudly at his fluttering streamer.
It swims in the wind, side by side with
those of Taro, his father,
and Aki, his mother. All three seem
carried by a great wave filled with love.

Joyful laughter is everywhere ...
for Naoki has grown bigger!

The Great Wave off Kanagawa by Katsushika Hokusai

Hokusai made *The Great Wave* as part of a picture series called *Thirty-Six Views of Mount Fuji*. You can also hear *The Great Wave* in a musical piece called *La Mer (The Sea)*, by French composer Claude Debussy. Debussy once said that Hokusai's colored woodcut inspired him to write this piece.

Color woodcut
25.9 x 37.2 cm
ca. 1830

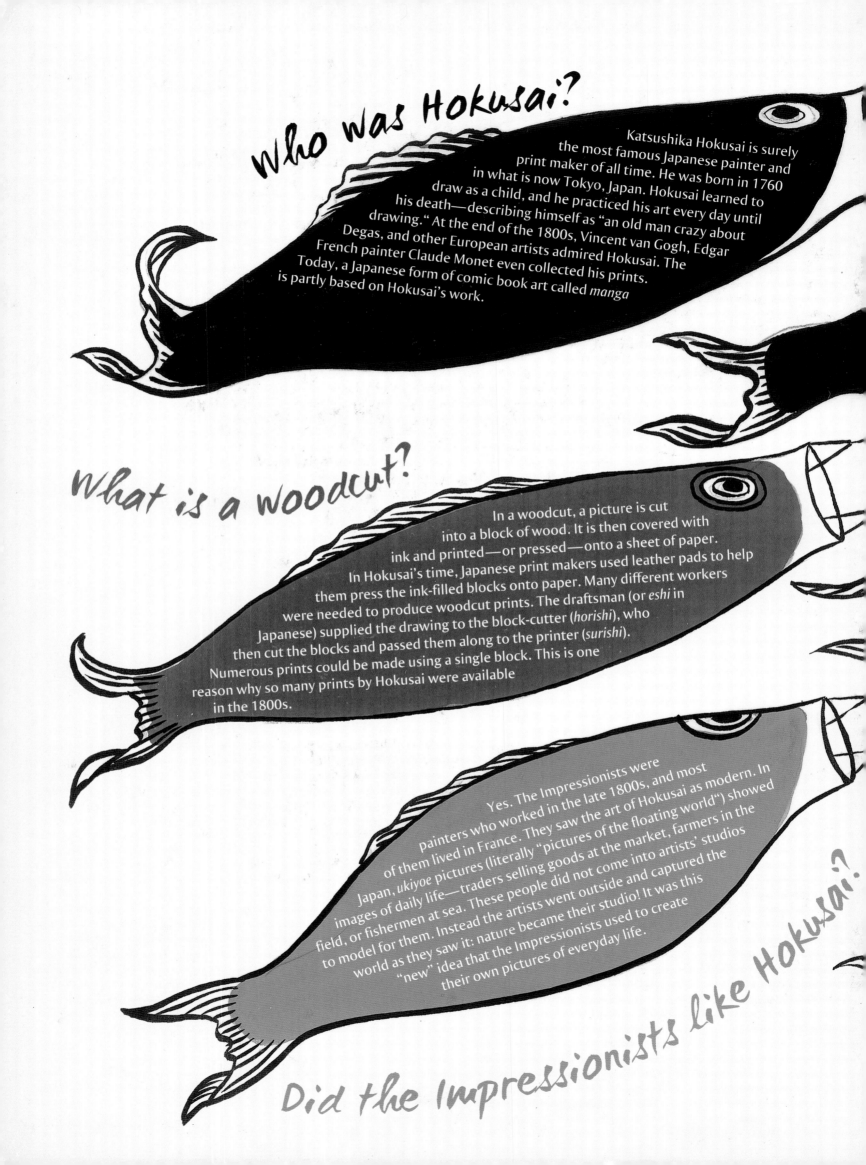

Who Was Hokusai?

Katsushika Hokusai is surely the most famous Japanese painter and print maker of all time. He was born in 1760 in what is now Tokyo, Japan. Hokusai learned to draw as a child, and he practiced his art every day until his death—describing himself as "an old man crazy about drawing." At the end of the 1800s, Vincent van Gogh, Edgar Degas, and other European artists admired Hokusai. The French painter Claude Monet even collected his prints. Today, a Japanese form of comic book art called *manga* is partly based on Hokusai's work.

What is a woodcut?

In a woodcut, a picture is cut into a block of wood. It is then covered with ink and printed—or pressed—onto a sheet of paper. In Hokusai's time, Japanese print makers used leather pads to help them press the ink-filled blocks onto paper. Many different workers were needed to produce woodcut prints. The draftsman (or *eshi* in Japanese) supplied the drawing to the block-cutter (*horishi*), who then cut the blocks and passed them along to the printer (*surishi*). Numerous prints could be made using a single block. This is one reason why so many prints by Hokusai were available in the 1800s.

Did the Impressionists like Hokusai?

Yes. The Impressionists were painters who worked in the late 1800s, and most of them lived in France. They saw the art of Hokusai as modern. In Japan, *ukiyoe* pictures (literally "pictures of the floating world") showed images of daily life—traders selling goods at the market, farmers in the field, or fishermen at sea. These people did not come into artists' studios to model for them. Instead the artists went outside and captured the world as they saw it: nature became their studio! It was this "new" idea that the Impressionists used to create their own pictures of everyday life.